If You Were There in 1776

Also by Barbara Brenner

If You Were There in 1492

If You Were There in 1776

Barbara Brenner

Bradbury Press *New York*

Maxwell Macmillan Canada *Toronto*
Maxwell Macmillan International
New York Oxford Singapore Sydney

Acknowledgments

This book could never have been written without the many experts willing to share their special knowledge with me. I'm grateful to Harold Gill of the Williamsburg Foundation for his thorough reading of the manuscript and to Cathy Grosfils, Audiovisual Editorial Librarian at Williamsburg, for helping me to visualize life in colonial America. The librarians at Marywood College, Scranton, and at Milford Library in Milford, Pennsylvania, were, as usual, fantastically dedicated. My husband, Fred, was a perceptive as well as patient sounding board. Special thanks have to go to my editor and friend, Barbara Lalicki, whose superb editorial eye was always a beacon and a comfort as I wandered through the labyrinths of history.

Copyright © 1994 by Barbara Brenner

All rights reserved. No part of this book may be reproduced or transmitted in any form or by any means, electronic or mechanical, including photocopying, recording, or by any information storage and retrieval system, without permission in writing from the Publisher.

Bradbury Press
Macmillan Publishing Company
866 Third Avenue
New York, NY 10022

Maxwell Macmillan Canada, Inc.
1200 Eglinton Avenue East
Suite 200
Don Mills, Ontario M3C 3N1

Macmillan Publishing Company is part of the
Maxwell Communication Group of Companies.

First edition
Printed and bound in the United States of America
10 9 8 7 6 5 4 3 2 1

The text of this book is set in Galliard.
The illustrations are reproductions of woodcuts, maps, and paintings of the period, as well as more recently completed drawings.

Library of Congress Cataloging-in-Publication Data
Brenner, Barbara.
    If you were there in 1776 / by Barbara Brenner.—1st ed.
        p.   cm.
    Includes bibliographical references and index.
    Summary: Demonstrates how the concepts and principles expressed in the Declaration of Independence were drawn from the experiences of living in America in the late eighteenth century, with emphasis given to how children lived on a New England farm, a Southern plantation, and the frontier.
    ISBN 0-02-712322-7
    1. United States—Social life and customs—1775–1783—Juvenile literature. 2. United States. Declaration of Independence—Juvenile literature. [1. United States—Social life and customs—1775–1783. 2. United States. Declaration of Independence.] I. Title.
E163.B78 1994
973.3—dc20   93-24060

Overleaf: The minutemen left their farms and families and went off to fight the British.

Contents

George Washington

John Adams

Molly Pitcher

Phillis Wheatley

Daniel Boone

Mercy Otis Warren

Benjamin Banneker

Paul Revere

Abigail Adams

Martha Washington

Here are a few of the men and women who helped make independence happen. You could have met some of them if you were there in 1776.

Benjamin Franklin

Benjamin West

George Mason

Thomas Jefferson

Patrick Henry

Thomas Paine

John Hancock

John Dickinson

Joseph Brant

Charles Willson Peale

You'll meet all of them in these pages.

Rebels in favor of independence tore down the British royal coat of arms on Independence Hall in Philadelphia.

People often ask writers where they get their ideas for books. This one started with the Declaration of Independence:

When, in the course of human events, it becomes necessary for one people to dissolve the political bands which have connected them with another . . . a decent respect to the opinions of mankind requires that they should declare the causes which impel them to the separation.

I got to wondering: What *human events* were the writers talking about? What *political bands* were they dissolving? What were those *causes* that impelled the separation? It seemed that the Declaration of Independence ought to be the hero of this story. But independence is only an idea. It needs flesh and blood heroes to make it come alive. In other words, who were those *one people*? What were they up to that famous year? Above all, how would it feel to be part of the "spirit of '76"?

Here is what I found out. . . .

Barbara Brenner

George III became king of Great Britain at the age of twenty-two. Never very stable emotionally, he eventually went mad.

The World in 1776

I t may seem sometimes as if 1776 was a strictly American year. But of course there was a whole world out there. It had around 700 million people in it. (That's about one-seventh of today's population.)

Napoleon Bonaparte was seven years old in 1776. Mozart was twenty, and his music was already world-famous. "Mad" George III was king of Great Britain. Louis XVI ruled France. On the science front, a Scottish engineer named James Watt had just invented a new steam engine. In the visual arts, Thomas Gainsborough and George Romney were the most popular living portrait painters in Europe. Mark Catesby was being remembered for his paintings of the animals and flowers of the American colonies.

Let's take a quick time-trip back to 1776 and see what life

was like. You'll find some things quite up-to-date. In many places you'll see imposing brick buildings and paved streets. You'll observe people carrying umbrellas, wearing bifocals, eating in public restaurants, and going to museums.

But in spite of these civilized touches, you'll soon discover that the eighteenth century has plenty of rough edges. Thieves, kidnappers, and murderers roam city streets. In the forests highwaymen lie in ambush to rob unwary travelers. Pirates prey on ships at sea. In fact, whole nations are committing acts that later will be considered crimes. They invade other countries, conquer people, gobble up their land and goods, and often enslave them. Spain has taken over huge chunks of South America, including what are now Paraguay, Uruguay, Argentina, and Bolivia. Great Britain rules over an empire that includes India, Canada, and

The Royal Academy of Art in London attracted crowds.

several Caribbean islands, as well as colonies in North America. Japan is so terrified of being taken over by the greedy Europeans that it has closed its borders altogether.

A particularly awful form of international trade is the buying and selling of people. People are being captured and sold into slavery by the tens of thousands. Almost the entire young population of some parts of Africa is disappearing.

No doubt about it. Individual rights are in short supply in 1776. But—something is brewing. Something new and radical. People are getting tired of being under the thumbs of princes, kings, queens, or emperors. It is dawning on them that they may have rights. This year there is a slave rebellion in southern Peru. Peasants are revolting in a part of what will become Czechoslovakia. There are rumblings of discontent in France, in Poland, in Greece. Suddenly words like *freedom, liberty,* and *independence* are on people's lips and are being talked about in many languages. A Frenchman, Jean-Jacques Rousseau, is saying that the only system of government worth having is one that everyone has a voice in and that leaves people as free as they were before.

Some people in England are even arguing with their own king. They think that George III ought to grant freedom to his American colonies.

Ah yes. Those American colonies . . .

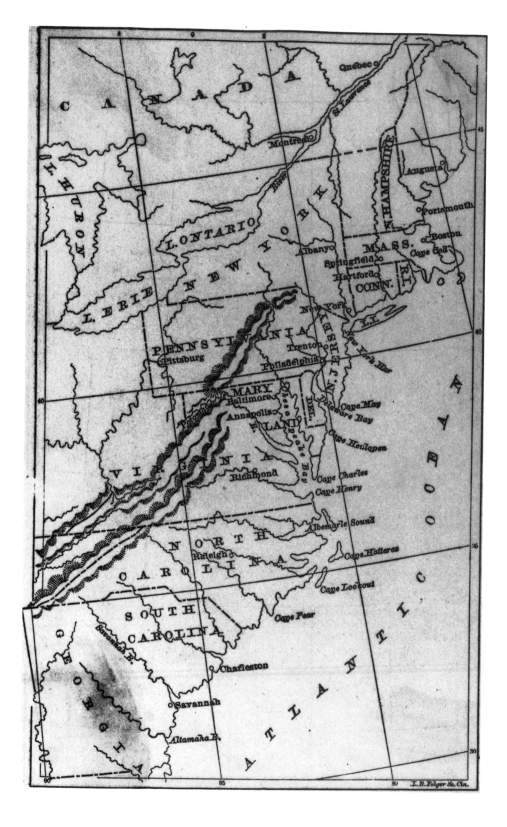

The Colonies

Altogether, there were approximately three million people in North America in 1776. (That's about the population of the present-day state of Iowa.) Around two million lived in thirteen British colonies in the eastern part of the country. In those days Massachusetts, Rhode Island, Connecticut, and New Hampshire were known as the New England colonies. New York, New Jersey, Pennsylvania, Maryland, and Delaware were called the Middle colonies. Virginia, the largest colony, was part of the section known as the South. So were North Carolina, South Carolina, and Georgia.

Imagine for a few minutes actually living in that time. What's it like? Let's say you live in a city. Even in the cities the wilderness is never far away. In some places you can see a wolf or a bear in your own backyard. In other places it's only a little way to a

The wilderness was never very far away.

forest where no tree has ever been cut down. It's said that a squirrel can hop from tree to tree for a thousand miles and never touch the ground. In fact, there are so many different kinds of trees in North America that some of them haven't even been named yet.

Rabbits, raccoons, deer, foxes, opossums, and chipmunks are part of your life. As for squirrels, some people eat them, other people keep them as pets, but most people think of them as pests. In the colony of Pennsylvania, for example, you'll actually be paid to shoot a squirrel.

In 1776 you can see birds that will become extinct, such as the Carolina parakeet and the passenger pigeon. You're able to watch ducks migrating in flocks as much as a mile wide and seven miles long. One writer says it looks like "a great storm coming over the water."[1]

Suppose you live near water. Imagine digging clams and oysters as big as a man's hand. Or catching a lobster as much as six feet long. There are so many salmon and shad that they're considered "trash fish" not worth keeping. Whales, too, are plentiful. Killing them is good business. Whalebone is used in corsets, and the blubber is a source of whale oil. In 1776 lamps all over the world are being lit with oil from whales harpooned by New England whaleboats.

Whaling was a hazardous occupation.

As for wild plants, some of them, like maize and potatoes, have been growing in North America since before the Indians arrived. Others have been brought from Europe for planting by travelers and settlers. The foreign plants have put down roots, just as the foreign settlers have.

The Europeans who originally settled here came from all over—from France, Germany, Holland, and Sweden as well as from England, Scotland, and Ireland. They started arriving around 1600. Some colonists left their homelands in style, with land grants from kings and plenty of money in their waistcoats.

By 1776 some families had been in the colonies for generations.

Others were on the run because of their religious or political beliefs. Many of these folks arrived with only the clothes on their backs. Another large group of people who came to the colonies were Africans who had been brought to the colonies against their will. Still other immigrants—young apprentices and skilled workers, as well as convicts, prostitutes, or homeless poor people—shipped to the New World as indentured servants, trading freedom for a chance to change their luck. Over half of the original settlers of the South and the Middle colonies came over in this way, bound by contract to a master without pay for a period of years and then given their freedom.

In 1776 Europeans are still coming to America. But some of the "first families" have been in the colonies for over a hundred years.

Wherever you live in the thirteen colonies, there are one or more colonies "next door." This doesn't mean that colonists are always good neighbors. In fact, your colony may fight with another colony over borders or land or business deals. You could even get the impression that the colonists don't care much for one another. Some New Englanders seem to think that Virginians are frivolous. Virginians often find Pennsylvanians rough. A great many people find New Yorkers vulgar.[2]

Still, you and the other European Americans of 1776 do have

some things in common. For the most part, you share a common background, culture, and language. In each of the thirteen colonies, there are the same classes of people—some wealthy landowners and businessmen, a few lawyers, doctors, and other professionals, and a large number of tradespeople, skilled and unskilled workers, and farmers. Farmers are the largest group everywhere, even on the frontier.

The thirteen also have similar governments. There's usually a royal governor, appointed by the king. The governors are supposed to have the final say on colonial matters. However, early on the colonies saw that many of the governors were either incompetent or not in touch with local issues. They have gotten into the habit of going around them. They make their own local laws and set local policy. Rhode Island has already outlawed slavery, and Virginia and Pennsylvania have done away with the death penalty except as punishment for capital crimes.

Meanwhile, even though they don't always get along, geography and common interests have brought the colonists together. There's brisk trade among them in rum, fish, rice, corn, molasses, indigo, tobacco, whale oil—and slaves. As they carry on their business, they trade news, information, and ideas. They talk politics. Locals meet with one another to discuss common problems.

For quite a while now, these meetings have been less about business and more about politics. Colonists have discovered that many of them dislike certain aspects of being a British colony. They share a dislike for many of the royal governors. They hate having to pay taxes to Britain without having any say in the matter. Furthermore, they resent paying taxes to a country three thousand miles away. They hate having ten thousand British soldiers on their soil and British sailors in their dockyards.

Every colony seems to have some of the same grievances against the "mother country." On that they can agree. They formed the first official Congress of delegates in 1774 to meet about these grievances and to petition the king. This organization has become stronger each year. This year all thirteen colonies support it. They now call themselves the United Colonies.

But the king doesn't seem to be paying attention. As a result, the grievance meetings of the Congress have turned into protests. Protest has turned into open resistance against British rule. Resistance has led to rebellion. And finally, rebellion has led to a shooting war.

At this point some colonists believe things have gone too far. Others don't think they have gone far enough.

That's the way it is in the colonies as the year 1776 begins.

The First Continental Congress was a forum for airing
grievances against the mother country.

In January of 1776 the "rebellion" was still unofficial. A delegation of colonial leaders had been meeting to decide what to do about it for more than six months. Among the delegates to this Second Continental Congress were some very famous names—John Adams and John Hancock of Massachusetts, Benjamin Franklin and John Dickinson of Pennsylvania, and Thomas Jefferson and Richard Henry Lee of Virginia. George Washington of Virginia had been a delegate, but had left in July of 1775 to assume a new job—General of the Continental army. It was a tough assignment. There wasn't even a government to pay an army.

The main problem seemed to be that not everyone wanted independence from their mother country. In fact, some people wanted independence from the Congress! Here's what these folks were singing:

> "These hardy knaves and stupid fools,
> Some apish and pragmatic mules,
> Some servile, acquiescing tools,—
> These, these compose the Congress!
> When Jove resolved to send a curse,
> And all the woes of life rehearse,
> Not plague, not famine,
> but much worse—
> He cursed us with a Congress."[3]

Five colonists were killed by British soldiers in the Boston Massacre, (1770)—Samuel Gray, Samuel Maverick, James Caldwell, Crispus Attucks, and Patrick Carr.

Rebels

▯▯▯▯▯▯▯▯▯▯▯▯▯▯

Rebellion was nothing new in the colonies. There had been incidents long before 1776. Not all of them were against Britain, either. From time to time, American tenant farmers had revolted against American landowners. Enslaved people had rebelled against their American masters. According to historian Howard Zinn, in the hundred years before 1776 there had been at least eighteen uprisings, six black rebellions, and forty riots in the colonies.[4]

The main fight, of course, was colonists versus Brits. If you were around back then, you would surely have heard of the Boston Massacre of 1770. In that riot five colonists, including a free black worker named Crispus Attucks, were killed by British soldiers. You might have been one of the ten thousand people who marched in the funeral demonstration for the victims. Three years later, in 1773, you might have helped dump tea into Boston Harbor to protest British import taxes.

Growing up in the colonies, you'd surely have known about King George's harsh laws, listened to grumbling about his awful taxes, and even seen with your own eyes those hated "lobsterbacks" in their red British uniforms. You could have known someone who was kidnapped to serve in the British navy. You might have heard rumors of a secret radical group, the Sons of Liberty, who were agitating to be free of England altogether.

In 1774 the members of several colonial governments formed the First Continental Congress. All thirty-two British colonies in America were invited but only twelve agreed to come. (The Canadian and Caribbean colonies sent a polite no, as did Georgia.)

This first Congress met in Philadelphia, and passed a resolution condemning British interference in colonial affairs. Patrick Henry made a stirring speech there, and ended by saying, "The distinctions between New Englanders and Virginians are no more. I am not a Virginian, but an American." A big step!

After that call to action, people began to take sides. From north to south, farmers and laborers, tavern keepers and lawyers, plantation owners and printers started to line up for or against independence from English rule and an English king. Those in

Patrick Henry was known for making great speeches.

favor of the king called themselves Loyalists, or Tories. The rebels opposed to the king and in favor of independence called themselves Patriots, or Whigs. In some families there were bitter arguments because some members were Tories and some were Whigs. A fair number of couples actually split up over politics. Others took a more practical approach. One partner went to England, one stayed in the colonies. That way, no matter how things shaped up, at least one family member would be on the winning side.

In 1775 Paul Revere took his famous ride. British soldiers and colonials fought their first pitched battles at Lexington and Concord, in Massachusetts. When King George heard about the fighting, he announced that he considered twelve of the American colonies "in full rebellion against the Crown."

One county in North Carolina promptly declared itself independent of England. The rebels approved. But most of the colonists were still hoping to resolve their difficulties with Britain. They just wanted to have a fairer relationship with the British Empire. At the same time, a few people who didn't know much about politics started to feel that their farms or land or businesses were threatened. They joined the rebels by enlisting in the Continental army or the local militia.

In the intervals between skirmishes, the colonists and their

British enemies spent their time annoying each other, and worse. If you were part of a Patriot family, you might have been one of the children throwing garbage or stones at the British soldiers. If your family supported the king, you could have been on the receiving end of some serious violence. Your home might have been broken into. Someone you knew who was a Tory could have been tarred and feathered, or ridden on a rail. You might have heard George Washington's famous remark about the Tories: "One or two have done what a great number ought to have done long ago—committed suicide."[5]

Being a Tory could be plenty uncomfortable in 1776.

War was a reality by the spring of 1775. Not only were colonial soldiers and militiamen killing Englishmen, they were killing one another. In one battle a regiment of North Carolina Scotch Highlander colonists loyal to the king fought a pitched battle against rebel colonists. However, by the beginning of 1776 Congress still hadn't been able to agree on an official statement breaking away from Britain and declaring war. Even General George Washington seemed to have had mixed feelings. Although he had given up toasting the king at official dinners, Washington's design for a new American flag included the crosses of England and Scotland. Clearly Washington hadn't entirely given up on the idea of being part of the British Empire!

Meanwhile, at the Second Continental Congress John Adams made a strong speech in favor of complete independence. John Dickinson opposed him. Dickinson and Adams had such a bitter fight that after that day they never spoke to each other again. Many delegates to the Congress maintained that the people they represented weren't ready for revolution. The time wasn't ripe. People needed to be persuaded. Dr. Benjamin Rush, a Pennsylvania delegate, suggested that a reporter named Tom Paine write something on the subject of independence. Paine wrote something. He called it *Common Sense*.

 Thomas Paine's little pamphlet, written in plain language, laid out the reasons why the colonists should be independent of England. It became the runaway best-seller of the year. Hundreds of thousands of copies were sold within a few months. Abigail Adams, John's wife, was so taken with its ideas that she wondered how "an honest heart, one who wishes the welfare of his country, can hesitate one moment at adopting them." George Washington said "*Common Sense* is working a powerful change in the minds of men."[6] He was right. Paine's words fired up the American Revolution and revolutions as far away as Poland, Greece, and France. There was even a rumor that King George had discovered his own son, Crown Prince George, reading *Common Sense*! Whether this really happened isn't known. But there's little doubt that *Common Sense* paved the way for the Declaration of Independence.

The Way They Looked

▯▯▯

L et's try to get a picture of those colonial Americans. Imagine yourself an average colonial child dressed in the clothes of that period. How would you have looked? Probably like a mini version of your mother or father. Children and adults dressed alike. For winter, boys and men usually wore knee breeches, a shirt, a vest, and a knit cap in cold weather. Girls wore loose gowns, bonnets, skirts, and woolen stockings. Underwear as we know it had yet to be invented.

There were no shopping malls in 1776. You couldn't watch for a sale and buy yourself some new clothes (spelled *cloathes* back then). Trousers and skirts were most often made at home, from scratch. Up north, winter clothes were likely to be *linsey-woolsey*—fabric woven of threads of linen and wool. It was a long wait for a new outfit. First the flax plant had to be grown,

Farm women made their own clothes.

Wealthy colonists wore the latest fashions from Europe.

makers sent their wealthy American customers dolls dressed in the latest styles. Often one of these costumed dolls became a plaything for a rich little girl—sort of a colonial Barbie doll.

Well-to-do men were just as interested in fashion as women. Men as well as women wore silk stockings, but it was the men who liked to show off their shapely calf muscles. If a man felt he was lacking in "leg appeal," he'd have his tailor sew a pad in his stockings to make a proper muscle bulge![7]

The sons of these men dressed like their fathers, in fancy velvets and ruffles. Imagine wearing this outfit, seen on one Boston businessman around this time: a velvet pea green coat, white vest, *small clothes* (buff or yellow cotton close-fitting knee breeches), white silk stockings, and pumps fastened with silver buckles. Those small clothes, by the way, might have been tied at the knees with ribbons that reached down to your ankles.

Girls wore tight corsets and hoopskirts. Black and blue was a fashionable color combination in 1776. Here's what twelve-year-old Anna Green Winslow wore to a party that year: a yellow coat, black bib and apron, a striped tucker (a frill of lace around the shoulders) and yards of blue ribbon around her neck. Silk or velvet shoes were the style for afternoon strolls in the city. But since the streets were usually muddy and dirty, women covered their shoes with galoshes.

As a final touch, a wig was powdered.

As for hats, brims had grown larger for years, until it was impossible to keep them from flapping. It became stylish to pin the brim back on one side, then the other. By 1776 a man's hat was pinned in three places, creating the famous tricorne.

The biggest fashion craze before the Revolution was the wig. It became more and more bizarre. Some women wore towering mounds of false hair, filled with puffs, feathers, and any number of fancy ornaments. Young girls cut off their own hair or shaved their heads so they could be fitted for a wig. Poor girls who needed money sold their hair to wigmakers. At the height of the wig craze, one Virginia father, William Freeman, paid nine pounds for a wig for his seven-year-old son. You can get some idea of how much this was when you realize that an average worker in those days made about twenty-five to thirty pounds a year.

Once you had a wig, a wig pick was a must. Wigs were so heavy and hot they made people's heads sweat. Sweat attracted lice. The pick was for removing those tiny visitors, since your wig was seldom washed.

George Washington enjoyed wearing fine clothes.

The War of Independence brought a distinct change in the fashion scene. It started with the Revolutionary leaders. George Washington exchanged his silver buckles and gold-embroidered waistcoats for a buff-and-blue Continental uniform that he designed himself. Benjamin Franklin and other Patriots gave up wigs and began to wear their hair long or in simple ponytails. Patriot women stopped wearing expensive and showy clothes. Martha Washington set an example for other wealthy women by making her own homespun dresses, reusing old silk stockings to add a note of color to her weaving.

However, some women found it hard to give up their interest in fashion entirely. So they invented a new hairstyle in honor of independence. It consisted of thirteen curls at the neck—one for each of the thirteen United Colonies!

In most households meals came to the table in one pot.

What's for Dinner?

E ven in perilous times, people have to eat. What would you have been eating in the colonies in 1776? Certainly not tomatoes. Very few colonists would take a chance on eating that "poisonous" fruit. Corn, however, was a different story. It was one food everyone ate. Without corn, it's doubtful that the settlers of North and South America would have survived. The Indians had taught them how to grow it and how to cook it. They had also introduced the settlers to potatoes, beans, squash, and pumpkins and to the mix of beans and corn that the Indians called succotash.

Most colonial women were too busy to prepare a new dish for each meal. So in a typical household, you ate the same thing day after day, until the supply ran out. In most of the thirteen colonies, it was a safe bet that the main dish would have corn in it. Corn came into the pot for breakfast in the form of corn-meal mush, sweetened with molasses. Hoecakes made of corn were a standard lunch. For supper there was corn pone, corn stew, or hasty pudding made with corn. Even apple pie was often made with a corn dough crust. As a treat there was—surprise!—popcorn. You can see why a poem by colonial writer Joel Barlow contains the line "All my bones are made of Indian corn." Colonial families also ate meat in many forms. Pork was especially popular since it could be smoked and salted down so that it wouldn't spoil.

Meals varied somewhat from place to place. There's a record of a Sunday dinner at the Adams house before the war that consisted of Indian pudding made of ground corn (corn again!), then a meat course of veal and bacon, neck of mutton, and vegetables.[8] There's no mention of dessert, but it might have been pie or fruit.

What did you wash your meal down with? Water was often too dirty for drinking. Everyone drank beer, wine, cider, or rum. A mixture of rum and cider, called "flip," was a popular drink, even for children. At the end of a meal, there was sometimes a cup of coffee or hot chocolate.

Children were expected to behave themselves at the table. A book of manners written around this time lays out the rules:

- *Don't sit down until the blessing is asked and your parents tell you to be seated.*
- *Don't ask for anything.*
- *Never speak unless spoken to.*
- *Break your bread; never bite into a whole slice.*
- *Never take salt with a greasy knife.*

Speaking of salt, if you were invited anywhere for dinner, it was polite to bring your own saltcellar. Salt was scarce in 1776, and it was a necessity for preserving meat as well as for cooking. (Salt was produced by evaporating it from seawater.)

Woods and fields were a source of meat for the table.

In fact, the fight for independence had some drastic effects on what people ate. Even before the war started, food began to get scarce. At one point the British blockaded the harbor of Boston so that no food could get in. A Bostonian complained, "It's pork and beans one day and beans and pork the next."[9]

In 1776 you would definitely not have been offered tea. Imported tea was a symbol of those hated British taxes. Most Americans had decided not to drink English tea for the duration. They substituted homemade raspberry tea or "liberty tea," made from the loosestrife plant. Many colonists also pledged not to eat mutton. Sheep were much more valuable alive. Their wool could be made into clothes for American soldiers.

Sheep were an important part of farm life.

In the early months of 1776, the members of the Second Continental Congress were working hard. But unlike the people in occupied cities, they were eating well. While Congress was in session, John Adams, Benjamin Franklin, and the other delegates were often wined and dined at the homes of wealthy Patriot friends or fellow delegates. At one of these sumptuous dinner parties, they had soup, oysters, fish, turkey, goose, chicken, molded jellies, plum pudding, cake, tarts, hot flip, and spiced punch!

Thomas Jefferson couldn't have been too pleased. He was a vegetarian.

Colonial farmers defended their land with whatever weapons they had.

Farmers

Farmers were the backbone of the thirteen colonies. In 1776 most colonists made their living farming. Even lawyers and other professionals owned farms and called themselves farmers.

Suppose you lived on a typical small farm. Here's a sample of what it would have been like:

Let's say your farm is in New Hampshire. Some member of your family has lived there since 1640, the year the colony was founded. Your great-grandparents built the farmhouse you live in. It's a simple, squarish house with a wing added on each end. Your grandparents built one addition. The other one is the new room your parents added after your sisters were born. None of the rooms are painted; it's considered extravagant to "lay your rooms in oil." Your house and the barn that's attached to it sit on a hillside surrounded by ten acres of ploughed fields. The rest of your land is forest.

You're New Englanders—Yankees, you call yourselves. And you're tough. You have to be. You live where the winters are cold and the soil is full of rocks. In fact, those walls that mark the boundaries of your property are made of stones that all came out of your own ground.

It's rocky on most New England farms. People joke that so little grows here that even a grasshopper can't find a square meal. Nevertheless you Yankees have managed, by hard work, to make your farms produce enough to live on and some to sell. You grow beans, apples, squash and pumpkins, turnips and potatoes. They're crops that can be kept all winter. Corn is your main crop. It keeps better than wheat and not a part of it goes to waste. You eat it on the cob and sell it, you dry it and have the kernels ground into flour. Then you feed the leaves and husks to the animals.

You probably have a domestic animal or two on the farm. When the pig gets fat, when the cow no longer gives milk, when the chicken doesn't lay, it winds up on your dinner table. When it comes time to slaughter a large animal, the meat is salted down, smoked, or pickled so it won't spoil. Every part of a cow or pig is used. The hide is tanned for leather. Bones are used for buttons. Fat makes soap. *Waste not, want not* is a New England motto.

Your farmhouse is out in the country, a few miles from a town. There are other farms nearby. All of them are grouped around "common ground." The church and the meetinghouse are there. Most of your social life centers around this tiny square. Parties and dances take place here. The common, or village square, is where people gather to talk. Once in a while, a peddler comes by and sets up his wares on the common. Everyone gathers around his wagon to buy what can't be had in town. Your mama can buy a *twiffler* or a *basin* from a peddler; that is, a pudding dish or a vegetable bowl.

Going to town is usually a family expedition. You go there for staples such as salt, sugar, and tobacco or to have the miller grind your corn into flour. Your father visits the blacksmith in town to get your horse shod. You can sell some of the produce from your farm in town and pick up your mail there. In the winter you bring things back and forth from town on a *pung,* which is a kind of sled.

Outside of these trips, it's mainly work, work, work. No sooner is one set of chores done, than another one comes up. It's a safe bet that you never say that you have nothing to do. On a small farm, there's always work for every member of the family. You and your sisters and brothers are very much part of the team. You'll work as hard as your parents do as soon as you can. And some of what you do actually brings in money for the family.

If you're a farm boy of about ten, a day's entry in your diary might read something like this:

> *Up at six. Fed the pigs. Brought in wood for the day. Went to school until four. Came home and was sent to gather vegetables. Sat down before supper to spool some yarn. After supper worked with my jackknife to cut some birch splinter brooms, which will bring six cents each. Father read the Bible to us. Went to bed eight o'clock.*

In another season you might tell of shucking and scraping corn, picking wild cherries for pies and jam, tying onions, collecting hog bristles to sell to the brushmaker, gathering nuts, and—in early spring—collecting sap from the maple trees and boiling it into syrup.

Not a minute is wasted. Even when a boy tends the cows in pasture, he doesn't just sit around. He does a bit of spinning on a hand distaff called a *rock*, or he knits. (Boys as well as girls were taught to knit.)

Everyone in the family pitched in to help with the chores.

Hunting was also part of boys' and men's work. You'd have hunted and trapped for the dinner pot. You would probably have bagged your own Thanksgiving turkey. And in 1776 you could have been one of the boys as young as thirteen and fourteen who shouldered a rifle or musket, lied about his age, and joined the militia.

What about farm girls? What were they doing that year? They had some of the same chores boys had. There were standard girl jobs as well. Girls plucked the feathers from geese, fetched water, cooked, and made soap and candles. As a colonial girl, you might have begun planting the seeds for your family's home garden when you were as young as four years old. You would have helped your mother collect eggs and sell produce at the town market.

You would surely have been spinning if you were big enough to stand on a footstool to reach the spinning wheel. Many women and girls did spinning and weaving at home for other people as well as for themselves. Often mothers and daughters worked at this cottage industry together. In 1776 you and your mother might have been making cloth for soldiers' uniforms. Sometimes families hired out their girl children to spin in other people's houses. To spin two skeins of linen thread was a good day's work. If you were "hired out," you would have made about eight cents a day besides your board and keep.

Girls' diaries of this time give a picture of their lives. Here's part of an account of one day written by a Connecticut girl named Abigail Foote:

Fixed gown for Prude . . . Mended Mother's Riding-hood . . . spun short thread, fixed two gowns . . . carded tow,* spun linen . . . hatcheled flax* with Hannah, we did 51 lbs. apiece, pleated and ironed, read a sermon . . . spooled a piece, milked the cows, spun linen . . . made a broom of guinea wheat straw . . . set a red dye . . . spun harness twine, scoured the pewter . . .[10]

---

*Tow was the coarse broken flax fiber prepared for spinning. Hatcheling was combing the flax fibers to separate them.

It sounds exhausting. But if you were there, you probably would have accepted your long day without question. Everyone worked. It was the way things were on family farms all over the colonies. And when boys and girls grew up and married, they used the skills they'd learned in their homes and taught them to their children, who in turn taught them to their children. And so on . . .

It wasn't hard to get New England farm families behind the movement for independence. The thought that British troops might try to take away their property set the men to cleaning their muskets and the women to making uniforms for the soldiers. In fact, the small farmers throughout the colonies were the heart of the armed resistance. They believed firmly in what the Declaration of Independence said, that everyone had the right to "life and liberty." Their land was their life and they wanted the liberty to use it as they saw fit.

The owners of large plantations lived a life of luxury.

Planters

Down south the weather was kinder. Farmers could grow things over a longer season. In colonial times tobacco was a staple crop in Virginia. In South Carolina it was mainly rice and indigo. In Georgia cotton was a main crop.

Staple crops were grown on *plantations*. Some of these plantations were small. Families did their own labor, or had one or two indentured servants. They raised their own vegetables and perhaps had a few sheep, pigs, or cows. They spun their own clothes and lived, in many ways, as they did on farms in New England or in the Middle colonies.

But there were also large plantations in the South. The one belonging to William Byrd of Virginia, for instance, covered 275 square miles. It was almost a quarter the size of the colony of

A small plantation in Maryland

Rhode Island. George Washington's plantation was so extensive that it had its own private wharf for shipping crops to market. Large plantations like these had their own churches and storehouses and schools and workers' cottages. Kitchens and laundries were in separate buildings, apart from the house. Often long driveways led up to huge mansions surrounded by exquisite gardens. Some of the mansions were modeled after the estates of English noblemen. Others looked like Greek temples.

Imagine living on one of these southern estates. Make believe for a few minutes that your home is on a tobacco plantation in Virginia and you're the child of the owner. Your house has imported Oriental rugs, French wallpaper, silver tea sets, and furniture made by the finest craftsmen in the colonies. You own a closet full of the latest fashions from Europe.

Carter's Grove, a famous Virginia plantation still in existence

Getting the tobacco to market was a job that involved both enslaved people and the owners of the plantation.

You're surrounded by luxury. You have private tutors, lessons in French, in dancing, in playing an instrument. You may be sent to Europe as part of your education. You and your brothers and sisters each have an enslaved person to wait on you. There are thirty more slaves who just take care of the house and grounds. Others work in the fields.

If you're a girl, you'll be trained to supervise the staff of house servants and to set an elegant table. By the age of ten, you already know how to embroider, to sing, and to play the harpsichord. You don't know how to cook, but you do know how to plan a menu. You are being taught how to keep the household accounts and to manage a plantation home like the one you're growing up in.

The men in your family don't plow the fields and plant the crops. Your father inherited the plantation from his father, who came from England with a land grant from the king. There is a "lieutenant," a manager who runs the plantation. Although your papa keeps close tabs on his business, he still has plenty of leisure time for activities like organizing hunting parties. He and your brothers "ride to hounds" a few times a week.

Your family enjoys entertaining. Guests from the next plantation or the next colony provide an excuse to party and dance, to show off new clothes, and to share elegant menus and rare wines. They also bring news of the outside world to the plantation. But plantations are often miles from one another and it gets lonely. When company is scarce, your father may send one of the house slaves down to the head of the road to watch for travelers and to invite them up to your house for a visit.

In those days guests could stay a day, a week, or a month. Offering hospitality was a matter of pride. However, once in a while a guest overstayed even a southern welcome. Thomas Jefferson's servants predicted that Jefferson's guests would send him to the poorhouse. Guests at Monticello would often stay for weeks, filling as many as twenty-six of his thirty-six stables with their horses and eating a whole cow every day or two.[11]

Not all plantation owners spent their time living like lords of the manor. Many southern landowners served in local colonial governments. A number of them, like Thomas Jefferson, played a vital role in the independence movement. But in spite of their deep interest in democracy and freedom, all of these wealthy planters were slave owners. Their gracious lifestyle was made possible to a large extent by the institution of slavery.

 Thomas Jefferson and George Washington were the most famous "southern gentlemen" associated with the Declaration and the War of Independence. But Arthur Middleton, Peyton Randolph, Richard Henry Lee, John Rutledge, George Mason, and many other gentlemen farmers participated in the Continental Congresses and helped frame the Declaration of Independence. In fact, some of the language of the Declaration comes directly from the constitution of the state of Virginia, which was written by George Mason. Some historians believe that this lesser-known document, which stresses individual rights, is as important as the Declaration of Independence itself.

New York Harbor in the eighteenth century

The Cities

Cities were the hub of life in the thirteen colonies. The largest cities—Boston, Newport, New York, Philadelphia, Baltimore, Charles Town (Charleston)—were all on water. They lay along the Atlantic coast like beads on a chain. The big cities had one thing in common—deep harbors. Trading ships could sail right up to the docks to unload their tea and silks, china and rum, and their cargoes of captured people. The boats could then be loaded with lumber and rice and indigo to take back across the ocean.

Big cities were the places to see the latest fashions, to enjoy the newest plays, and to hear the hottest political news and gossip. However, like the thirteen colonies themselves, each city had its own individual stamp. Want to see for yourself? Then hop aboard for an imaginary trip.

You'll travel down the coast by stagecoach. The Flying Machine, a flashy blue-and-red vehicle, is state-of-the-art public transportation right now. It carries people and mail, follows a set route, and picks up and drops passengers and letters at various stops. It runs on real horsepower—a team of six horses. The horses are switched at certain "stages" in the journey. (That's why it's called a *stagecoach*.) The actual Flying Machine took ten days just to go from Boston to New York. But for your trip this fine May day it will really fly!

Boston, Massachusetts

First stop is Boston. Like most big cities, Boston is a place of contrasts. It has neighborhoods of stately, elegant wood and brick houses. At the same time it has seamy slums. Across the river there's a college (Harvard) that is over a hundred years old. Boston is also home to rough, tough street gangs like the North and South Enders. These two groups have been fighting each other for years. But this year they've declared a truce and banded together to fight the British.

At first glance, you might say they've been successful. There are no British soldiers to be seen in Boston this spring day. However, the credit for this belongs largely to General George

With the help of fifty-nine cannons supplied by General Knox,
Washington was able to break the British blockade of Boston Harbor.

Washington and his able general Henry Knox. In March Knox sneaked men and heavy guns to the heights of Boston and took the British completely by surprise. The rebels have been in control of the city ever since.

As your coach passes the docks, you get wind of one of the city's principal occupations—fishing. You see the codfish piled up on the dock. You glimpse the rotting carcass of a whale. Whaling boats still go out from all the northern port cities, but Boston is particularly noted for its whaling ships and sailors.

The city air is pretty foul—a mixture of garbage, rotting fish, produce from the street markets, and a few smells you try not to identify. It's no wonder that John Adams, who has a law office in Boston, claims that the "air of the town of Boston is not favorable."

In the streets of Boston you can see "mechanicks" at work, making barrels, laying bricks, building ships, or doing dozens of other jobs.

Your Flying Machine goes around Boston Common—a sort of park in the middle of the city. It's "common ground" that everyone can use. Farmers graze their cows there. At dusk the shepherd boys will blow their horns to call the cows home. They blow a different set of notes for each herd. As each farmer's cows hear "their" sound, they leave the Common and start for home.

There are dozens of taverns in Boston. Some of them have recently changed their names and their signs to honor the War of Independence. You watch one tavern owner change his sign from KING GEORGE to GEORGE WASHINGTON.[12]

Taverns were favorite places to eat, drink, and gossip or talk politics. Many taverns were run by women.

The stagecoach stops to pick up passengers at the Green Dragon Tavern, a favorite gathering place. Here, as everywhere, the talk is all about the war, the Congress, and when the colonies will declare themselves for independence.

Boston was widely known as the most rebellious city in the colonies. It was the scene of the Boston Massacre and the Boston Tea Party and was considered to be the heart of the independence movement. Boston was among the first cities to advocate breaking away from Great Britain.

Newport, Rhode Island

You touch down briefly in Newport, Rhode Island. It's very different from Boston. Smaller. No grand public buildings. The only architecture of note is a Jewish synagogue, the oldest one in colonial America. Jews settled in Newport a long time ago. It's odd that they're still not allowed to vote here, since Rhode Island has a reputation for religious tolerance.

There's no college, seminary, or museum in Newport. But there are newspapers. One of them, the *Newport Mercury*, is published by a woman, Ann Smith Franklin. She's Benjamin Franklin's sister-in-law.

Opposite page: The Touro synagogue in Newport is the oldest Jewish house of worship in America.

The State House, Newport, Rhode Island

The whole colony of Rhode Island is fiercely independent and has been since it was founded in 1663. Unlike most of the other colonies, Rhode Island's charter allows it to elect its own governor.

If fishing is the biggest business of Boston, shipbuilding is probably the largest industry in Newport. In fact, Rhode Island was the first colony to suggest the idea of building a Continental navy. The first naval ships were built here. They sailed out of Newport Harbor in February. By all accounts they are doing a good job of harassing the British at sea.

Smuggling and privateering may be the next largest occupations in Newport. Officials and customs officers look the other way when illegal cargoes sail into Newport Harbor. It may seem strange to you that a city in a colony that has outlawed slavery within its borders still traffics in enslaved people and other illegal cargoes.[13]

The whole colony of Rhode Island stands behind the War of Independence. You stop at a tavern in Newport, where they're singing a song about Washington:

"To Washington's health,
Fill a bumper around,
For he is our glory and pride.
Our arms all in battle
With conquest be crowned,
Because he's on our side."[14]

When Congress finally got around to writing a declaration of independence, Rhode Island offered its own colonial charter as a good model. In fact, it was a ready-made "declaration." All that was needed, according to Rhode Islanders, was to take out any mention of the king.

New York, New York

When you're in New York City, you can tell you're on an island. Almost every street faces water. On one side is the Hudson, on the other the East River. These days the view isn't pleasant—there are British ships laying offshore in every direction.

You can feel the war all around in this city. The streets are crowded with Continental soldiers and militiamen. General Washington himself is here, preparing to defend New York against the British attack that everyone is sure will come.

Strolling the streets, you hear the sound of foreign languages and see many people of color. More than 15 percent of New York's 18,000 residents are Africans. Most of them are slaves.[15] The names Stuyvesant, Dyckman, Gansevoort remind you that

New York was originally settled by the Dutch.

You stay in New York overnight—time enough to pick up some city survival skills. You buy clean drinking water from a street vendor. You make sure that you know where the fire buckets are at the inn where you're staying. Fire is a real danger everywhere in 1776; it's particularly so in cities. (The most disastrous fire in colonial history will break out in New York in September. It will destroy a large section of the city.)

The worst part of New York is the noise. People shout to make themselves heard over the cries of chimney sweeps, peddlers, tinkers, grinders, and ragmen. If you talk with some New Yorkers, you may find yourself agreeing with John Adams about their conversation. "They talk very loud, very fast and altogether. If they ask you a question, before you can utter three words of your answer, they will break out upon you again and talk away."[16]

You can escape the babble of New York easily. From city to country is no more than a walk up the Broadway. Here even the war seems remote. You can go turtle fishing from the shore, then cook up your catch and have a picnic. Young couples finish off the evening by crossing the Kissing Bridge, which is well named.

New York City was a hotbed of radicals. When the Declaration of Independence was first read out loud in the public square, there was a riot. Mobs tore down a huge gilt-covered statue of King George, stripped it of its gold, and dragged away its two thousand pounds of lead to make musket balls for the Continental army.

King George's statue

A Philadelphia street

Philadelphia, Pennsylvania

Next stop, Philadelphia. It's the capital of the New World—the largest city in the colonies, and the second largest city in the whole British Empire.

Philadelphia seems extremely well planned. The streets are all well lit with whale oil lamps and are patrolled by security guards for safety. The avenues are laid out in a sensible grid pattern with paved areas on either side. Philadelphians call these "walkways for foot passengers." You call them sidewalks.

Benjamin Franklin was one of Philadelphia's most famous citizens. This portrait was done by his friend and fellow Patriot, Charles Willson Peale.

A river, the Schuylkill, runs through the heart of the city. As your stagecoach passes by, you see a few people boating. But a huge number of young men are marching in practice military drills in the parks and public squares. From the looks of things, the "City of Brotherly Love," founded by the peaceful Quakers, seems ready for war.

Riding through Philadelphia, you catch a glimpse of the first hospital in the colonies, and the two public libraries started by Benjamin Franklin. There's also a science museum, which is said to contain the skin of a rattlesnake twelve feet long. Another tourist attraction is the State House. It's the only State House in the colonies that has apartments for Indian chiefs to stay in when they come on official business. At this moment Philadelphia has other claims to fame. Benjamin Franklin's daughter's house has been turned into a shirt factory, where women are making shirts for the rebel soldiers. And—of course—the Second Continental Congress is meeting here.

No American city was more associated with liberty and the Declaration of Independence than Philadelphia. But the city did have its Tories. According to historical accounts, in 1776 there were over one thousand people in Philadelphia who were opposed to independence.[17]

Baltimore, Maryland

Breezing south, you begin to notice different kinds of trees and flowers. As you approach Baltimore (named for its founder, Lord Baltimore), you begin to see horse farms. Horse racing is a popular sport in the colonies and many of the horses are bred on Maryland horse farms.

As you get to the heart of the city, you see a number of handsome Catholic churches. They reflect the fact that Baltimore has a larger population of Catholics than other colonial cities. The city also has the best natural harbor of all the colonial ports. The water is over thirty-five feet deep for more than forty miles around Baltimore Harbor. That has made it a great international port.

Shipping grain, tobacco, indigo, and other products grown elsewhere in the colonies is Baltimore's main industry. But it's also known for the ships built there. You pass a shipyard where men are at work on a trading vessel. A little further down the

street you look in on a rope maker's shop. In this place they make ships' ropes up to a hundred fathoms (six hundred feet) long.

In some ways Baltimore doesn't seem as advanced or as well kept as the other cities you've visited. There's still no college in the whole colony. (The closest thing to a college is King William's Free School in Annapolis, which will become St. John's College in 1784.) Young women flock to Baltimore. Perhaps it's because there's a rumor that Maryland, and Baltimore in particular, is the best place in all the colonies for a young woman to find a husband.[18]

The common people of Baltimore were solidly behind independence. Still, at the end of May 1776, Maryland delegates kept changing their minds about whether to vote for a break with Great Britain. John Adams was annoyed with them. He referred to Maryland as "so eccentric a colony—sometimes so hot, sometimes so cold; now so high, then so low."

Maryland finally did come around and vote for independence. In fact, a Baltimore printer, Mary Katherine Goddard, was chosen by Congress to print the official copy of the Declaration of Independence.

Opposite page: Baltimore had the deepest harbor in the colonies.

Charles Town, South Carolina

Your last port of call is Charles Town. A city of 12,000 people, it lies on a peninsula between two rivers. Charles Town is a city with a distinct French flavor—the most elegant city in the colonies. Nothing you've seen matches its style in public buildings and grand houses. As for luxury, there is so much wealth in Charles Town that some residents have two homes—one on their plantations in the country and one in Charles Town city proper. They come here in the summer to escape the heat of the lowlands.

It doesn't take long to realize that this city has two faces. In the evening you see Charles Town's cultural face. You go to the Dock Street Theatre and see a performance of Shakespeare's *Othello*. The next morning your stagecoach passes the slave market and you see the barbaric spectacle of a slave auction. The enslaved people will soon be standing up to their knees in muck in the fields, farming the rice that keeps rich Charles Town residents in finery.

Yet in Charles Town, too, there are people of learning and conscience who support freedom and independence. At the moment, the city is preparing for battle. The British are bound to attack soon because of Charles Town's strategic location. You

Charles Town Harbor

see Continental soldiers and civilians on the streets building barricade walls of palmetto leaves bolstered with sand. Some Patriots are taking the leaden weights from the windows of their houses so they can be cast into musket balls for the soldiers.

A few months ago, you wouldn't have seen so much support for the war in Charles Town. But by now most of the Tories have been driven out of the city.

The colony of South Carolina declared itself independent of Britain in March of 1776, three months before the Declaration of Independence was written. However, most of the wealthy planters of Charles Town were not known as political radicals. Many rebels felt that Charles Town residents signed on for independence when it was good for their pocketbooks.

The Declaration

I t was June of 1776. In Philadelphia the roses were in bloom in backyard gardens. But the delegates to the Continental Congress had no time to smell the roses. They were still arguing over whether to declare the colonies independent. The stuffy meeting room echoed with angry words. John Adams had tried to understand his colleagues' lack of agreement. He admitted that it was "hard to get thirteen clocks to strike at the same time." But now, John Adams was losing patience. So was Richard Henry Lee of Virginia. Lee said they ought to "call the revolution a Revolution and get on with it." John Dickinson of Pennsylvania disagreed. He said that would be like "destroying our house in winter . . . before we have got another shelter." And so it went.

A committee was chosen to draft a declaration of independence. Left to right: John Adams, Robert Livingston, Roger Sherman, Thomas Jefferson, Benjamin Franklin

If you were near the State House during those momentous days, you might have caught a glimpse of some of the delegates. You could have seen Benjamin Franklin catching a little fresh air on the back path. You might have seen John Adams on the steps, holding forth with Robert Livingston and Roger Sherman. He would probably have been talking about the new committee to which they had been appointed. They were supposed to come up with a declaration of principles that all the thirteen colonies could agree to. No small task!

You might also have seen a tall, red-haired young man around the State House—Thomas Jefferson. Jefferson, the plantation owner, was also a lawyer. At thirty-three, he was one of the youngest—and brightest—delegates to the Second Continental Congress. He had been appointed to that committee, too, along with Benjamin Franklin. Jefferson had been chosen to write the declaration because everyone agreed that he was the best writer.

If you could have peeked into the second-floor window of a certain rented room on Market Street, you might have seen Tom Jefferson scratching away with his quill pen. He would have been seated at a small wooden desk that he had designed himself. He might have had his pet mockingbird sitting on his shoulder.

How did Jefferson begin? Where did he get his ideas? He must have done a good bit of reading. It appears that for starters, Jefferson looked at other things that had already been written on the subject of freedom and independence. Among the documents that he looked at were Tom Paine's *Common Sense*, the Virginia Bill of Rights, and John Locke's *Two Treatises on Government*. With these pieces of writing for reference, he got a beginning statement down on paper. It was eighty-six words long. After having set the tone for his prose, Jefferson went to work in earnest. Within a week, he had a rough draft of a declaration.

Thomas Jefferson's first draft of the Declaration of Independence was subjected to some editing.

He presented his work to the other committee members for their comments. Franklin and Adams and Jefferson himself were tough editors; altogether they made forty-eight changes. After that the document was ready for the Congress to approve it. But before the Congress could vote on the declaration itself, it first had to agree to a resolution saying that the United Colonies

Independence Hall was buzzing on the eve of July 4, 1776.

"were and of right ought to be independent." The date to debate that question was July 1.

On the appointed day, John Adams made a speech in favor of independence. But when his speech was over, there were only nine votes in favor of independence! New York abstained. Pennsylvania was opposed. South Carolina defected. And Caesar Rodney, the crucial delegate from Delaware, had gone home to take care of his sick wife.

At Ben Franklin's urging delegates in favor of independence got busy behind the scenes in the Congress. The two Pennsylvania delegates who were opposed agreed not to vote at all. That guaranteed Pennsylvania three *yea* votes. Then Caesar Rodney of Delaware arrived and voted yea. South Carolina followed. New York's delegate, Robert Livingston, was opposed, but he abstained instead of voting nay. Final vote: twelve for independence, none opposed.

Opposite page: When Congress voted for independence, Robert Livingston of New York abstained so the vote could be unanimous.

On the third of July, the Congress started debating the Declaration of Independence itself. Jefferson had written a passage against slavery that took up more than a fourth of the declaration. It upset nearly everyone to some degree. South Carolina and Georgia put their collective feet down. They wouldn't approve the Declaration if the antislavery passage stayed in. It was dropped.

There were other changes as well, but finally the Declaration was approved. On July 4 John Hancock, president of the Continental Congress, and Charles Thomson, secretary, signed it. It was a solemn moment. Everyone knew that by this act they were committing treason. Benjamin Franklin probably voiced the sentiments of the delegates when he said, "Now we must all hang together, or assuredly we shall all hang separately."

IN CONGRESS, JULY 4, 1776

The unanimous Declaration of the thirteen united States of America.

When in the Course of human events, it becomes necessary for one people to dissolve the political bands which have connected them with another, and to assume among the powers of the earth, the separate and equal station to which the Laws of Nature and of Nature's God entitle them, a decent respect to the opinions of mankind requires that they should declare the causes which impel them to the separation.

We hold these truths to be self-evident, that all men are created equal, that they are endowed by their Creator with certain unalienable Rights, that among these are Life, Liberty and the pursuit of Happiness.— That to secure these rights, Governments are instituted among Men, deriving their just powers from the consent of the governed,— That whenever any Form of Government becomes destructive of these ends, it is the Right of the People to alter or to abolish it, and to institute new Government, laying its foundation on such principles and organizing its powers in such form, as to them shall seem most likely to effect their Safety and Happiness. Prudence, indeed, will dictate that Governments long established should not be changed for light and transient causes; and accordingly all experience hath shewn, that mankind are more disposed to suffer, while evils are sufferable, than to right themselves by abolishing the forms to which they are accustomed. But when a long train of abuses and usurpations, pursuing invariably the same Object evinces a design to reduce them under absolute Despotism, it is their right, it is their duty, to throw off such Government, and to provide new Guards for their future security.— Such has been the patient sufferance of these Colonies; and such is now the necessity which constrains them to alter their former Systems of Government. The history of the present King of Great Britain is a history of repeated injuries and usurpations, all having in direct object the establishment of an absolute Tyranny over these States. To prove this, let Facts be submitted to a candid world.

He has refused his Assent to Laws, the most wholesome and necessary for the public good.

He has forbidden his Governors to pass Laws of immediate and pressing importance, unless suspended in their operation till his Assent should be obtained; and when so suspended, he has utterly neglected to attend to them.

He has refused to pass other Laws for the accommodation of large districts of people, unless those people would relinquish the right of Representation in the Legislature, a right inestimable to them and formidable to tyrants only.

He has called together legislative bodies at places unusual, uncomfortable, and distant from the depository of their Public Records, for the sole purpose of fatiguing them into compliance with his measures.

He has dissolved Representative Houses repeatedly, for opposing with manly firmness his invasions on the rights of the people.

He has refused for a long time, after such dissolutions, to cause others to be elected; whereby the Legislative powers, incapable of Annihilation, have returned to the People at large for their exercise; the State remaining in the mean time exposed to all the dangers of invasion from without, and convulsions within.

He has endeavoured to prevent the population of these States; for that purpose obstructing the Laws for Naturalization of Foreigners; refusing to pass others to encourage their migrations hither, and raising the conditions of new Appropriations of Lands.

He has obstructed the Administration of Justice, by refusing his Assent to Laws for establishing Judiciary powers.

He has made Judges dependent on his Will alone, for the tenure of their offices, and the amount and payment of their salaries.

He has erected a multitude of New Offices, and sent hither swarms of Officers to harrass our people, and eat out their substance.

He has kept among us, in times of peace, Standing Armies without the Consent of our legislatures.

He has affected to render the Military independent of and superior to the Civil power.

He has combined with others to subject us to a jurisdiction foreign to our constitution, and unacknowledged by our laws; giving his Assent to their Acts of pretended Legislation:

For Quartering large bodies of armed troops among us:

For protecting them, by a mock Trial, from punishment for any Murders which they should commit on the Inhabitants of these States:

For cutting off our Trade with all parts of the world:

For imposing Taxes on us without our Consent:

For depriving us in many cases, of the benefits of Trial by Jury:

For transporting us beyond Seas to be tried for pretended offences

For abolishing the free System of English Laws in a neighbouring Province, establishing therein an Arbitrary government, and enlarging its Boundaries so as to render it at once an example and fit instrument for introducing the same absolute rule into these Colonies:

For taking away our Charters, abolishing our most valuable Laws, and altering fundamentally the Forms of our Governments:

For suspending our own Legislatures, and declaring themselves invested with power to legislate for us in all cases whatsoever.

He has abdicated Government here, by declaring us out of his Protection and waging War against us.

He has plundered our seas, ravaged our Coasts, burnt our towns, and destroyed the lives of our people.

He is at this time transporting large Armies of foreign Mercenaries to compleat the works of death, desolation and tyranny, already begun with circumstances of Cruelty & perfidy scarcely paralleled in the most barbarous ages, and totally unworthy the Head of a civilized nation.

He has constrained our fellow Citizens taken Captive on the high Seas to bear Arms against their Country, to become the executioners of their friends and Brethren, or to fall themselves by their Hands.

He has excited domestic insurrections amongst us, and has endeavoured to bring on the inhabitants of our frontiers, the merciless Indian Savages, whose known rule of warfare, is an undistinguished destruction of all ages, sexes and conditions.

In every stage of these Oppressions We have Petitioned for Redress in the most humble terms: Our repeated Petitions have been answered only by repeated injury. A Prince, whose character is thus marked by every act which may define a Tyrant, is unfit to be the ruler of a free people.

Nor have We been wanting in attentions to our British brethren. We have warned them from time to time of attempts by their legislature to extend an unwarrantable jurisdiction over us. We have reminded them of the circumstances of our emigration and settlement here. We have appealed to their native justice and magnanimity, and we have conjured them by the ties of our common kindred to disavow these usurpations, which, would inevitably interrupt our connections and correspondence. They too have been deaf to the voice of justice and of consanguinity. We must, therefore, acquiesce in the necessity, which denounces our Separation, and hold them, as we hold the rest of mankind, Enemies in War, in Peace Friends.

We, therefore, the Representatives of the united States of America, in General Congress, Assembled, appealing to the Supreme Judge of the world for the rectitude of our intentions, do, in the Name, and by Authority of the good People of these Colonies, solemnly publish and declare, That these United Colonies are, and of Right ought to be Free and Independent States; that they are Absolved from all Allegiance to the British Crown, and that all political connection between them and the State of Great Britain, is and ought to be totally dissolved; and that as Free and Independent States, they have full Power to levy War, conclude Peace, contract Alliances, establish Commerce, and to do all other Acts and Things which Independent States may of right do.— And for the support of this Declaration, with a firm reliance on the protection of divine Providence, we mutually pledge to each other our Lives, our Fortunes and our sacred Honor.

Button Gwinnett
Lyman Hall
Geo Walton.

Wm Hooper
Joseph Hewes
John Penn

Edward Rutledge

Thos Heyward Junr.
Thomas Lynch Junr.
Arthur Middleton

John Hancock

Samuel Chase
Wm Paca
Thos Stone
Charles Carroll of Carrollton

George Wythe
Richard Henry Lee
Th Jefferson
Benja Harrison
Thos Nelson jr.
Francis Lightfoot Lee
Carter Braxton

Robt Morris
Benjamin Rush
Benja Franklin
John Morton
Geo Clymer
Jas Smith
Geo Taylor
James Wilson
Geo Ross

Caesar Rodney
Geo Read
Tho M:Kean

Wm Floyd
Phil Livingston
Frans Lewis
Lewis Morris

Richd Stockton
Jno Witherspoon
Fras Hopkinson
John Hart
Abra Clark

Josiah Bartlett
Wm Whipple
Saml Adams
John Adams
Robt Treat Paine
Elbridge Gerry
Step Hopkins
William Ellery
Roger Sherman
Samel Huntington
Wm Williams
Oliver Wolcott
Matthew Thornton

John Hancock was the first person to sign the Declaration of Independence. He said he would sign it large enough so that King George could read it without his glasses. He became so famous for the signature that today we still refer to signing a paper as "putting your John Hancock on it."

The Declaration wasn't signed by any of the rest of the delegates until August 2. By that time many of the original fighters for independence had gone home. They didn't sign until much later. One delegate signed on as late as 1781 and seven of those who were present to vote for it never signed the Declaration at all.

On September 9, 1776, the United Colonies officially became the United States.

Opposite page: You can't miss John Hancock's bold signature on the Declaration of Independence.

Religion

░░░░░░░░░░░░░░░░░░░

Religious liberty was something most colonists already had. Freedom of worship was part and parcel of colonial life. By 1776 there were more than 3,000 religious groups. Although most colonists in the thirteen were Protestants, there were also Roman Catholics, Anglicans, some Moravians, Mennonites, and Shakers, and about 2,500 Jews. There was even a church in Pennsylvania that welcomed followers of Islam.

As a Protestant you could be Congregationalist, Presbyterian, Baptist, Quaker, Dutch Reformed, German Reformed, or any one of a dozen other denominations. One visitor to Philadelphia wrote that "in one house and one family four, five and even six sects can be found."[19]

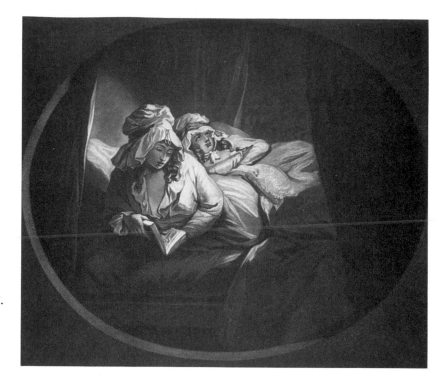

Stories from the Bible were often bedtime reading.

Some Christian sects were more strict than others. If you came from one of the stricter groups, you would have been forbidden to do many things that others allowed—dancing, for instance. The least strict sect was the Deists. They believed in an informal religion that simply accepted a Divine Creator. Benjamin Franklin, Thomas Jefferson, and George Washington all considered themselves Deists. None of them attended church regularly or took part in religious observances.

But most people did. Your family would most likely have prayed before and after each meal. Almost every household had at least one copy of the Bible and people knew it chapter and verse. If there was no church nearby, families often had an informal service at home. The family Bible and other religious books would be brought out and everyone would take a turn reading.

Religious education started early. *The New England Primer* was the first book many children read, and its stories were from the Bible. You would probably have learned to read with such questions as:

Who was the first Man? (Adam)
Who killed Goliath? (David)

Jews observed their Sabbath on Saturday, but the official Sabbath in the colonies was Sunday. On that day stores and businesses were closed. Even enslaved people and indentured servants had Sunday off. As a child, you wouldn't have been allowed to go fishing or play games on Sunday. In New York City, there was a special cage set up for boys caught fooling around on the Sabbath.

Religious leaders, like everyone else, took their stand on the question of independence, and they weren't necessarily in agreement. One Protestant leader, Rev. Jacob Durke, pleaded with Washington to quit the Continental Congress and to urge it to rescind the "hasty and ill-advised" Declaration of Independence.[20] At the same time, Rev. John Peter Muhlenberg left his Protestant church to join the Continental army. A Jewish leader named Francis Salvador declared, "There is a time to pray and a time to fight," and went off to join the militia.

 Thomas Jefferson and the other writers of the Declaration understood that not everyone in the colonies had the same religious feelings. They seem to have deliberately chosen language that would be acceptable to Jews and Deists as well as to Protestants and Catholics. For example, there's no mention of Jesus in the Declaration. And God is never called by name directly. Instead, there are references to *Nature's God,* the *Creator,* the *Supreme Judge,* and, in the final paragraph—*Divine Providence.* It's clear that this wording was no accident.

The Founding Fathers wanted to use language that would be acceptable to as many denominations as possible.

At Play

🁢🁢🁢🁢🁢🁢🁢🁢🁢🁢🁢🁢🁢🁢🁢🁢

As a child you might have had a little more playtime in 1776. Many schools were closed because of the war. So what might you have been doing for fun? Rolling hoops, blowing soap bubbles, and playing marbles were all favorite pastimes of children. In winter you might have been sledding or ice-skating. That summer you might have played hide-and-seek, tag, or chuckers. (The object of chuckers was to stand a distance away and "chuck" a penny or a stone into a hole.)

Most young children had only a few toys—a top, a whistle, a ball, a doll. Toys were often made at home, but could also be bought at a store or from a peddler. An older boy in 1776 usually carried a jackknife, which was a handy carving tool as well as a toy. Boys sometimes played football. It wasn't much

Opposite page: Grown-ups and children played games like tag and leapfrog.

like today's game but some parents in 1776 thought it was too rough, just as some parents do today.

Girls played with dolls made from rags or straw, corncobs, or wood. If your family was wealthy, you might have owned a fashion doll (see p. 28).

(see p. 28)

What about grown-ups? How did they "play"? In small towns and settlements, there were hunting parties for men and quilting bees for women. Neighbors often got together to watch cockfights and to bet on them. Wrestling contests and tugs-of-war provided rough-and-tumble competition at local fairs and holiday celebrations.

A few men played golf. A great many played at *boules*, which was a form of lawn bowling. Billiards was a favorite game in the

taverns. Outdoors, footraces were popular. So were pitching horseshoes and a similar sport, pitching the bar.

Barn raising, harvesting, and cornhusking were jobs that neighbors often did together. When the job was done, it was time to party. Everyone would bring food, someone would bring a fiddle, and the crowd would be off, dancing to a polka or a gallop.

Dancing was favored by high society, too. At a fancy party, a violin and other instruments were hired for entertainment and there was dancing far into the night. If you peeked in on most elegant parties in 1776, you would have seen several male guests in the buff-and-blue uniforms of American officers. A few Tory families still invited British soldiers to parties, but in 1776 they would have kept that activity very quiet.

Singing was entertainment for rich and poor, young and old. People sang every kind of song—lullabies, hymns, bawdy songs, drinking songs. Although there were no radios or CD players in 1776, just about everyone knew the words and tune to certain songs—like "Yankee Doodle."

Most well-educated Americans could play an instrument and read music. George Washington played the flute. Thomas Jefferson played the violin, and practiced for several hours every day. He was one of the first people in the colonies to own a piano.

The right to the "pursuit of happiness" is guaranteed in the Declaration of Independence. That idea was bound to have appeal to the colonists, since they valued good times and "pursued" them energetically.

Nor did they give up the pursuit when the war came. In 1776 Americans simply combined their good times with patriotism. Dances acquired special names in honor of the War of Independence. People danced to "Burgoyne's Surrender," "The Campaign Success," or "Clinton's Retreat." Instead of traditional drinking songs, they sang anti-British songs such as "The Dying Sergeant" and "The British Light Infantry," both written in 1776.

Arts and Crafts

If you lived back in 1776, many things in your house would have been handmade—the weather vane on the roof, the carved wooden bowls, the patchwork quilt on the bed, the painted chest in the corner. By that time these homely objects would have acquired a plain American "style" that reflected the spirit of simplicity and equality that went along with independence. Rebel colonials didn't want the things around them to look English or "royal." They turned their backs on fancy curlicues on furniture and silver the way they rejected flounces and frills in fashion. Today these simple colonial designs are considered valuable works of art.

There were a good many professional artists among the rebels. Take Paul Revere, for example. He was a silversmith and engraver by profession. Usually you could have found him making

Opposite page: A folk art portrait of George and Martha Washington done in a type of calligraphy called fraktor

silver teapots and fruit bowls or engraving bookplates. But he was never too busy to do a job for the Patriots. Revere took part in the Boston Tea Party, and was a secret agent and express rider for the rebel cause.

Paul Revere's silver designs are still being copied.

This self-portrait shows Charles Willson Peale in the natural history museum he started after the Revolution.

Charles Willson Peale was another artist with good rebel credentials. If you were a Patriot and looking to have your portrait painted, Peale would surely have been your number-one choice. You would have liked the fact that he wasn't a society painter. In fact, Peale had been a harness maker. He started painting portraits after having only two lessons in art.

Peale was a close friend of many of the Revolutionary leaders and signers of the Declaration. He painted portraits of Benjamin Franklin, Thomas Jefferson, and John Adams. He was Martha Washington's favorite painter; she chose him to paint her portrait and commissioned several portraits of George. But after the Declaration was signed, Charles Willson Peale decided he could be more useful to the cause fighting than painting. In August of 1776 he joined the militia as a common soldier.

Now—if you had a notion to become an artist yourself, Benjamin West might have been your role model. West developed a passion for drawing as a boy in Pennsylvania. With homemade

Some young artists used the stone floors for drawing.

brushes and colors, he managed to teach himself to draw and paint. It wasn't long before people began to talk about the young man who was painting such extraordinary pictures. A group of colonial businessmen interested in art paid to send him to Europe to study.

West stayed in England, where he became a famous painter and teacher and a close friend of King George III. He spent a great deal of time with the king, but never made any secret of his sympathy with American independence. He remained in touch with rebel leaders before and during the Revolution. Benjamin Franklin was the godfather of one of Benjamin West's children.

By a strange coincidence, Benjamin West was at the royal palace on the very day when the Declaration of Independence was first read to King George III. A friend later asked West how the king had reacted. According to Benjamin West, King George said, "If they can be happier under the government that they have chosen than under mine, then I shall be happy."[21]

Niagara Falls was part of the frontier.

The Frontier

What about the frontier? What was it like in 1776? Picture it. No roads. No houses. Just miles of trackless forest, plains and mountains, and crystal-clear rivers with Indian names—Shenandoah, Cayuga, Mississippi, Ohio.

Land was cheap on the frontier. All you had to do was head away from "civilization." Find a piece of land, and it could be yours. It was like a dream. Almost anyone could seek a fortune on the frontier. Few settlers stopped to think about the people who had named those rivers and who had hunted on that land for thousands of years. They pushed on, in some cases acquiring thousands of acres of land from the Indians in exchange for a few trinkets. The Indians usually didn't fully understand these exchanges since the whole idea of "owning" land was foreign to them.

In 1776 many people were picking up stakes and moving closer to the frontier, or to what some people called "the back-country." They were heading north and east to the Maine territory. They were going west to less developed parts of Vermont, New Hampshire, Connecticut, and Pennsylvania. Wisconsin was being settled by the English, Utah and Nevada by Spaniards. French fur traders were paddling up *les rivières* to settle parts of Canada. That year Daniel Boone led a party of settlers to the Kentucky territory.

Suppose, for a few minutes, that you're on that westward trek. What is it like?

First of all, you'll have to travel some to keep up. It's said that Dan'l Boone can walk 150 miles a day and that he knows every inch of the trail.[22] He has escorted hundreds of settlers through the wilderness to Boonesboro, Kentucky, the settlement named after him. It makes sense to travel with such a man.

The end of the trail is no more than a clearing in the middle of a forest. There are a few people and mules. Not much else. Your father quickly makes a cabin as a temporary shelter. It's made of logs and has an earthen floor and a bark roof. The windowpane is paper, coated with hog grease to let in a little light. A bear could easily put a hole through that window. You wonder if it will even keep out the wind and rain, let alone the

A band of pioneers being escorted into western country by Daniel Boone

99

animals. First things first, your father may tell you. He's busy helping the other men build a stockade against Indian attack.

For the time being, your whole family eats, sleeps, works, and plays in one room. You have one table—a rough board—and there are no chairs. The family eats Indian-style, sitting on the floor or on tree stumps. All seven of you sleep in two beds on corn husk mattresses you brought with you.

The boys and men get busy right away girdling the trees. A cut a few inches deep is made in the bark all around each tree. That kills the tree and is easier than cutting it down. Soon you'll have more sun coming into your cabin and more open space to plant crops.

Until you plant, food is hard to come by. You and the other children go out digging roots and looking for wild greens, nuts, and berries. The men and boys shoot rabbits and birds. In the fall you'll help set traps for beavers and foxes. The fur will be sold to traders in exchange for tools and other necessities.

Danger and discomfort are part of life on the frontier. On the discomfort side are the mosquitoes, fleas, ticks, and chiggers. As for danger, it comes in many forms. Wolf packs stalk the livestock. Poisonous snakes live in the woodpile. There are unfriendly Indians and unknown diseases. If anyone is hurt or gets sick, there's only do-it-yourself medical help.

Schools in frontier towns are few and far between. However, if kids can't go to school, some frontier parents bring school to the kids. Whatever books are in the cabin (the Bible is usually there) double as beginning readers. In the evening after work, Mama or Papa drills you in your "letters."

In many ways frontier children grew up very different from the children in cities and towns. Frontier boys and girls were wilder and tougher. A good many of them drank whiskey and took snuff, as their parents did. Many girls hunted and trapped along with the boys, and wore homespun jeans and moccasins. They were as strong as the boys, and needed to be. Sometimes the nearest clean water was a distance away and it was often the girls who carried the buckets back and forth.[23]

Everyday life on the frontier in 1776 was definitely not like life in *Little House on the Prairie*. It was an earlier time and a rougher one. Frontier people lived with constant stress. Fights erupted all the time. A friendly argument could change in a flash to a pitched battle and then to a killing. Being far from colonial courts, settlers took the law into their own hands. Vigilante "Regulators" patrolled the countryside, and their "justice" was likely to be quick and dirty.

The stressful life on the frontier often took its toll. Men and women broke under the strain. They became depressed and suffered "nervous afflictions." Diseases swept through settlements and left people without family. A few families gave up the frontier altogether and went back to where they'd come from. Others pushed on even further west, to what they thought would be a better settlement. But most people stuck it out, living in hope that next year, or the year after, things would get better.

In fact, for many frontier families it did. They actually found the good life that land speculators and scouts like Daniel Boone promised them. But wherever they settled, the frontier colonists changed the wild places. They timbered the trees for houses and furniture, wagons and barrel staves, and for open space for planting crops. They hunted and killed animals by the thousands for the fur and feathers that fetched such good prices. They disrupted animal habitat by establishing permanent homes on Indian hunting grounds. Still, in those days no one worried about the environment. If there were fewer animals and plants of a certain kind, it was hardly noticed. In 1776 no species seemed endangered.

 The people who lived on the frontier were not particularly involved with the Declaration of Independence or the rebel cause at first. They had made their own declaration of independence by moving to the frontier. Most of them wanted to be free of any government, British or American. Fighting the Revolution was actually forced on them. Out there it was a different war—a "border war"—fomented by the British. According to contemporary historian Page Smith, the British often paid Indians to murder frontier settlers.[24] These raids had little military value for the Brits. They were a way of punishing the Americans who were most remote from military support from the Continental army. However, these actions by the British stirred up hatred for the Indians among the colonists and left bad feelings that lasted long after the war was over.

The Indians

There were more than a dozen separate Indian nations living in North America in 1776. They went by various names. Back then you would have heard of the Iroquois, Algonquin, Sioux, and others. Each of these nations was made up of tribes, such as the Naticks, Penobscots, Cheyennes, Cherokees, Creeks, Mohawks, Seminoles, and Delawares. Each

Customs varied from tribe to tribe. Some Indians lived in tipis.

tribe or group spoke a different language. Each one had different customs. You certainly couldn't say exactly what Indian was, any more than you could say exactly what an American colonist was.

It was hard for the Indians and settlers to understand each other. Each group thought the others' ways were strange. For example, the colonists wondered why the Indians wore so few clothes and why they bathed so often. The Indians wondered why the colonists wore so many clothes and bathed so seldom.

As time went by, the two groups influenced each other. The settlers learned that it was better to use land to plant corn than to grow silk. They saw the usefulness of moccasins and buckskin leggings, and began to wear them. They learned to eat pemmican on the trail and succotash at home. For their part some Indians adopted colonial dress. A few converted to Christianity and went to schools set up for "savages." One Indian, Caleb Cheeshateaumuck, earned a bachelor's degree from Harvard. But he was an exception. Most Indians stuck with their tribal teachings and traditions. They lived in tipis or wigwams, wickiups or longhouses. Often they moved from place to place with the seasons. They had their own gods, and wore their own distinctively embroidered or decorated tribal clothing. What did change was the amount of territory the Indians had available. It became smaller and smaller.

Wigwams were covered with animal skins, bark, or rush mats.

In spite of the great land grab, some Indians remained friendly to the colonists. Some of the framers of the Declaration had Indian friends. The Cherokee warrior and orator Ontacette, for example, was a friend of Thomas Jefferson. The chief stayed with Jefferson at Monticello whenever he came to Williamsburg, Virginia. And John Adams would often stop at the wigwam of a Neponset Indian family he knew and be treated to peaches, apples, or plums from their fruit trees.[25]

The Native Americans lost ground every year. The question was—Who had the right to be on the land, those who had lived there for ages or those Johnnys-come-lately who had moved in?

That question clouded all relations between the colonists and the Indians. It led to bloody battles. Indians would wipe out a group of colonists. Colonists would burn out an Indian village. If you were there in 1776, you might have lived through Cherokee attacks along the whole southern frontier.

Occasionally in Indian raids, a settler's child would be taken captive by Indians. Imagine for a few moments what that would have been like:

You would probably have been adopted by the tribe. From then on your life would have been very different. To begin with, you'd have been more comfortable. Instead of itchy linsey-woolsey clothes and ill-fitting shoes, you'd have been wearing soft deerskins and very few clothes, or none at all. You'd have been eating more vegetables than you did at home. When you ate meat or fish, it would have been fresh, or dried, not salted or pickled, like the meat at home.

There would have been no school, at least not in the way you knew it. A girl would have helped cook and tend the crops. She would have learned how to make a tipi and skin a deer. A boy would have been taught to hunt and fish and to make and use a bow and arrow. You'd have learned how to stalk prey and how to ride a horse bareback. You might have worn bracelets and beads for the first time.

Some young captives seemed to enjoy life as Indians more than their former lives as colonists. Maybe it was because Indian mothers and fathers were generally not as strict as colonial parents were. They didn't train their babies by forcing them to stand and walk, or by taking food away from them. They didn't hit their children or lock them up in dark places for punishment as many colonial parents did. Girls in many tribes—the Iroquois, for example—had equal rights and could be warriors.

It was an open secret that many children who were captured by Indians didn't want to be rescued. Benjamin Franklin once wrote about these captured children: "When white persons of

Young boys learned how to tame wild ponies.

either sex have been taken young by the Indians, and lived awhile among them, tho ransomed by their friends . . . yet in a short time they become disgusted with our manner of life, . . . and take the first good opportunity of escaping again to the woods, from whence there is no reclaiming them."[26]

In 1776 most colonists hated Indians. Even Thomas Jefferson, who had friends among the Indians, refers to them in the Declaration of Independence as "merciless savages." The rights of Americans spelled out in the Declaration were never meant to apply to Native Americans. Some Indian tribes, such as the Mohawks and Senecas, saw the Revolution as a chance to get back at the people who had robbed them of their historic ground. These tribes joined with the British. Other tribes, like the Delawares and Stockbridge Indians, who had good relations with their colonial neighbors, helped the Americans. Still other tribes fought on one side of the Revolution only because their traditional tribal enemies were on the other.

TO BE SOLD on board the Ship *Bance-Island*, on tuesday the 6th of *May* next, at *Ashley-Ferry*; a choice cargo of about 250 fine healthy **NEGROES**, just arrived from the Windward & Rice Coast. —The utmost care has already been taken, and shall be continued, to keep them free from the least danger of being infected with the SMALL-POX, no boat having been on board, and all other communication with people from *Charles-Town* prevented.

Austin, Laurens, & Appleby.

N. B. Full one Half of the above Negroes have had the SMALL-POX in their own Country.

Advertisements for slave auctions ran in local papers.

Enslaved People

In the South you would have been surprised to find any large farm or plantation that didn't have slaves. One Georgia minister said that an enslaved population was "as necessary . . . as axes, hoes, or any utensils of agriculture."[27] George Washington had over a hundred enslaved people on his farm, although he disapproved of the slave system and called it "a cruel and unnatural trade."[28]

Imagine being a slave on that Virginia plantation we talked about earlier. Here's how things would have been for you:

You would have been a prisoner for life. You'd never be paid for your work. You could never leave your job. You could be sold at any time, like a cow or a pig. You wouldn't even have owned your own body.

Tobacco was an enormously profitable crop.

Your whole life would have centered around tobacco. You would most likely have been a "field hand." (A surprising number of girls and women as well as boys and men did heavy fieldwork.)

You'd have worked all day, every day, except for Sunday. April was planting time for tobacco. After the crop was planted, there was hoeing, weeding, cultivating. You'd have worked outside all through the hot southern summer. In August you and the other workers would have cut the tobacco plants and hung them in a shed to dry. Six weeks later the dry leaves would have been stripped from the plants and packed in hogsheads for shipping to market. The boys and men loaded the hogsheads onto wagons. Each one weighed over a thousand pounds. You would have gone home each day exhausted.

In 1776 you would probably have lived with your parents. Most slave owners at that time encouraged family life. They had discovered that people worked better if they weren't separated from their loved ones. Because a master owned any children of a female slave, slave owners wanted enslaved women to have husbands and children.

"Home" would most likely have been a poorly furnished one-room shack. One described in an inventory of a Virginia property around this time had "one bed, a few chairs, one iron cook pot, one brass kettle, a frying pan, iron pot hooks and a beer barrel."[29]

But even with one or two pots, your mother and father might have managed to cook tasty meals. Cooking was an important part of African tribal culture. Both men and women cooked and traditional recipes were passed down to boys as well as girls. Your parents, or their parents, would have brought with them remembered ways of making gumbos, jambalayas, and other dishes from their native regions. They would have adapted them to the meats and vegetables available in America and taught them to you. In fact, much of what we call "southern cooking" was originally created by the house slaves of colonial America.

Enslaved people in the South usually were a small, separate community. If you lived in this community, you would have worked and played with other enslaved children. You might even have attended a field school with white children and played with them until you reached a certain age. In 1776 in some places you would have been allowed to learn to read and write. Later this right was taken away.

Slavery was not confined to the southern states. Over four thousand black people lived in Massachusetts, according to a census taken in 1776. In all the thirteen colonies, people of color represented 20 percent of the non-Indian population. Although some of these black men and women were free, most of them were not.

In spite of hardships, some enslaved people managed to break out of their condition. They became mechanics and carpenters who were "hired out" by their masters and allowed to keep some of the money they made. In this way a few were able eventually to buy their freedom, or were freed voluntarily by their masters.

A number of these free men and women learned to read

On Sunday enslaved people were allowed a day of recreation.

and write and became well-known in various professions. One person you would certainly have heard of back then was Phillis Wheatley. Wheatley had been taught to read by her mistress, who later freed her. Phillis Wheatley became a poet; her patriotic verses were extremely popular in 1776.

Benjamin Banneker was another distinguished man of color. Banneker's grandmother, a freed slave, taught him to read. He went on to become an inventor, writer, and astronomer. Benjamin Banneker was a close friend of Thomas Jefferson—close enough to criticize Jefferson for some of his ideas about black people. Banneker told Jefferson, "You should wean yourself from those narrow prejudices that you have imbibed."[30]

Enslaved people were very much aware that a war of independence was being fought. They hoped it might result in some new freedoms for them. Some slaves tried to join the Continental army, but in 1776 Washington hadn't yet agreed to accept enslaved people or free blacks in his army.

Frustrated at being kept out of the fight for independence, some slaves escaped from their masters and joined the British, who promised them freedom after the war.

 How did the author of the Declaration stand on the issue of slavery? As we know, Thomas Jefferson was a slave owner himself. On the other hand, he did introduce a bill to free Virginia's slaves as early as 1769. And his original draft of the Declaration contained a paragraph denouncing slavery and blaming King George for that institution in the colonies. It was an unfair accusation, but it does show that Jefferson had mixed feelings about slavery. As you've seen on page 80, the final version of the Declaration never mentioned slavery. It didn't include enslaved people as being "endowed by their Creator with certain inalienable rights."

Nevertheless, the ideas in the Declaration did have their effect on the lives of enslaved people. Shortly after the Declaration was signed, the first enslaved blacks began to sue for freedom. According to historical records, no enslaved person who actually went to court was turned down.[31] However, very few African-Americans could afford to go to court even if they knew about the law. It has already taken more than two hundred years to make the Declaration apply fully to all Americans. And we're still working on it.

On July 9, 1776, the Declaration of Independence was read before
Washington's Army in New York.

The War

Once the Declaration of Independence became official, the war became official. The people of the thirteen colonies must have been worried by the awesome step they had taken. George Washington was certainly worried about his army. He needed to bolster their fighting spirit, so he ordered the Declaration read to them. Then he gave them a personal pep talk, in which he is reported to have said, "The General hopes that this important event will serve as fresh incentive to every officer and soldier to act with fidelity and courage . . . knowing that now the peace and safety of his country depends solely on the success of our arms."[32]

What was it like, living during a revolution? Imagine shortages of everything: money, food, clothing, even paper. Rags were collected house-to-house to make paper for documents.

Army dispatches had to be sent loose because envelopes were so scarce. Continental militiamen roamed the streets, stripping the lead gateposts from the houses of known Tories to make musket balls for their weapons. If you lived in British-held territory, you could have seen the hated redcoats invading local farms and plantations to scavenge for food.

Imagine your own family—a father or older brother—going off to fight. Sometimes the war came even closer. You could hear guns from your own front porch or watch a battle from your rooftop. Picture the horror of seeing families beaten or shot by soldiers, children wounded by the shelling of a town, or the mass graves of men shot down in battle.

For people who believed in the War of Independence, choices weren't simple. How much were you willing to give? A little money? Your fortune? Your job? Or your life? Some rich men bought their way out of their obligation to serve the cause or hired an indentured servant to go into the army for them. Some poor people joined up for the pay. But staunch Patriots of every class enlisted. Boys as young as twelve joined the militia or the Continental army. They were usually put to work as drummers or cooks' helpers. A few, like fourteen-year-old Theophilus Sargent, sneaked into combat by lying about their ages.

The soldiers you would have seen in 1776 were part of the strangest army ever. They were recruits from all over and from every class. One of Washington's officers was a blacksmith. John Dickinson, a delegate to the Second Continental Congress and an upper-class farmer-lawyer, was a private. Each army unit dressed in its own style and built its own style of barracks, depending on where the men came from. In the militia officers and enlisted men who knew one another were on a first-name basis, and ate and drank together.

The most experienced fighters in the army were the back-woodsmen of Virginia, Pennsylvania, and Maryland. They shot with rifles instead of the muskets used by the regular Continental infantry. These guns were heavier and longer than muskets. They

Opposite page: The volunteers were of different ages. Younger boys were usually assigned to be drummers.

were usually made by the owner, and each rifleman poured his own bullets and shaped them to fit his piece. Every man seemed to be a crack shot.

American newspapers made sure the British knew about these backwoods sharpshooters in buckskin shirts. One paper said, "The worst of them will put a ball into a man's head at the distance of 150 or 200 yards . . . therefore advise your officers . . . to settle their affairs in England before their departure."[33]

Some women took a direct part in the war by disguising themselves as men and joining up. Other women traveled with the soldiers and were paid a small sum by the army. These

Molly Pitcher firing a cannon

women were called camp followers, but don't get the idea that they were colonial "groupies" chasing after men in uniform. They did much more than follow their husbands or boyfriends. They took care of the wounded. They helped cook. They mended uniforms. In some cases they even went into battle with the men and helped load and fire the guns.

One of the most famous camp followers became known as Molly Pitcher. Her husband was killed in battle in 1776. She immediately took his place and continued to fire his cannon, even after she was wounded in the chest and had her arm almost completely blown off.

Women who stayed at home also did their part. The Daughters of Liberty collected money and made clothes for the soldiers. They made no secret of their feelings about the British. Here's part of a letter Mercy Warren wrote to a British soldier:

"Tea I have not drunk since last Christmas, nor bought a new cap and gown since your defeat at Lexington; and what I never did before, have learned to knit . . . I know this, that as free I can die but once; but as a slave I shall not be worthy of life. I have the pleasure to assure you that these are the sentiments of all my sister Americans."

There was spying by both sides in the fight for independence. Enemy and friend looked alike out of uniform, so it was hard to tell one from the other. A Boston businessman could be a spy for Britain, while a soft-spoken housewife might be carrying messages for the Continentals.

Plots and counterplots were the order of the day. In 1776 a plot was hatched to capture George Washington and to turn him over to the British. Thomas Hickey, one of Washington's guards, was involved. He was captured, tried, and put to death. Thomas Hickey was eighteen years old.

Children, too, worked as "secret agents." They were perfect spies since no one suspected them. If you were there in 1776, you could have been one of these children. You might have carried messages to a neighboring town to report a British troop movement. At the time you might have thought of it as a game, but it was deadly serious work. A young woman named Emily Geiger managed to eat up the letter she was carrying when she was captured. Nathan Hale, a Connecticut schoolmaster, was not so lucky. He was captured behind British lines and hanged without a trial. His last words are a dramatic part of 1776: "I only regret that I have but one life to give for my country."

 The signing of the Declaration of Independence was the beginning of a long, hard fight. By the end of the year 1776, things looked bad for the Americans. The British had won some key areas. Cities were under martial law. Some towns were under siege and had no food at all. Two-thirds of the American army had quit. According to some reports, the remaining men were hungry and sick. The British claimed that most of the rebel army had been defeated and that Washington had lost an arm in battle. The rumor wasn't true, but it had a bad effect on colonial morale. There was talk of replacing Washington as general. Tom Paine summed up the general mood in December of 1776 in his pamphlet *The Crisis*. He wrote, "These are the times that try men's souls."

But in spite of everything, the ideas of the Declaration held. The spirit of '76 refused to be quenched. As Washington said, "The spirit of freedom beats too high in us to submit to slavery."[34]

The rest is history.

Notes

ロロロロロロロロロロロロ

1. Many early naturalists, including John James Audubon, wrote of the tremendous numbers of wildfowl. Audubon described them as "darkening the skies." The quote here by an unnamed observer is from *Life in Colonial America*, by Elizabeth George Speare.

2. According to Page Smith (See Vol. 1. *A New Age Begins: A People's History of the American Revolution*), the speech and manners of colonists from one part of the country were fair game for ridicule by another.

3. The author of this Tory ballad is unknown. It is reprinted in *The American Heritage Book of the Revolution*, edited by Richard Ketchum.

4. According to Howard Zinn's *A People's History of the United States*, colonial ferment started in 1676 with Bacon's rebellion in Virginia. Much of the conflict, according to Zinn, pitted the poor against the rich.

5. See *Voices of the American Revolution*, edited by the People's Bicentennial Commission.

6. Ibid.

7. A tour guide at Williamsburg offered this bit of history. She further

explained that the expression "putting your best foot forward" came from the habit colonial gentlemen had of showing their legs when standing for a portrait.

8. John Adams ate a typical plain New England diet. He would have observed the ban on mutton in 1776. See *Chapters from the American Experience* by Frank M. and Marie L. Fahey.

9. See Vol. 1, *Life in America*, by Marshall Davidson.

10. See *Home Life in Colonial Days*, by Alice Morse Earle.

11. Ibid.

12. See *Life in Colonial America*, by Elizabeth George Speare.

13. Newport was known for its smugglers and privateers. See Vol. 1, *A New Age Begins: A People's History of the American Revolution*, by Page Smith.

14. From *Ballads of the Revolution*, Folkways Records.

15. See *A People's History of the United States*, by Howard Zinn.

16. See Vol. 1, *A New Age Begins: A People's History of the American Revolution*, by Page Smith.

17. This was out of a population of about 20,000. Ibid.

18. Ibid.

19. See *A Restless People: Americans in Rebellion 1770–1787*, by Oscar and Lilian Handlin.

20. See *George Washington: The Pictorial Biography*, by Clark Kinnaird.

21. It's odd that the king would have made this statement at the same

time that he was at war with the colonies. Perhaps George III said it out of respect for his friend Benjamin West. The exchange is chronicled in *America's Old Masters*, by James Flexner.

22. Daniel Boone was once asked whether he had ever been lost. He is reported to have replied, "Can't say I was ever lost but I was bewildered once for a few days." From *Life in America*, Vol. 1, by Marshall Davidson.

23. From *Founding Mothers*, by Linda Grant DePauw.

24. See Vol. 1, *A New Age Begins: A People's History of the American Revolution*, by Page Smith.

25. Ibid.

26. Ibid.

27. From *Daily Life: Sourcebooks on Colonial America*, edited by Carter Smith.

28. Ibid.

29. See *Founding Mothers*, by Linda Grant DePauw.

30. See Howard Zinn's *A People's History of the United States*.

31. From Vol. 1, *A New Age Begins: A People's History of the American Revolution*, by Page Smith.

32. Quoted in *The American Heritage Book of the Revolution*, edited by Richard Ketchum.

33. From Vol. 1, *Life in America*, by Marshall Davidson.

34. From *Voices of the American Revolution*, edited by the People's Bicentennial Committee.

Sources

The information in this book came from many sources, including the following historic sites: Colonial Williamsburg, Jamestown, and Old Sturbridge Village; the Gettysburg and Yorktown battlefields; cemeteries and historic houses in Pennsylvania, New Jersey, and New York; the Hagley Museum and restoration in Wilmington, Delaware; Middleton Place Plantation and the old city of Charleston, South Carolina; and the harbor restorations at Baltimore, New York, and Mystic, Connecticut.

One set of books I found especially helpful was Page Smith's two-volume *A New Age Begins: A People's History of the American Revolution*. Much of the detail on children's lives came from the venerable but still valuable source *Home Life in Colonial Days* by Alice Earle and *Child Life in Colonial Days* by the same author. *Founding Mothers* was an especially good source of information about the lives of colonial women, African-Americans, and Indians. *The Spirit of 'Seventy-Six* provided authentic firsthand reports of the time.

Here's a complete bibliography:

Bailey, Thomas A. *Probing America's Past*. Lexington, Mass.: D. C. Heath, 1973.

Bank, Mirra. *Anonymous Was a Woman*. New York: St. Martin's Press, 1979.

Boorstin, Daniel J. *The Americans: The Colonial Experience*. New York: Vintage Books, 1958.

Bremner, Robert H., ed. *Children and Youth in America*, Vol. 1. Cambridge: Harvard University Press, 1970.

Commager, Henry Steele, and Richard B. Morris. *The Spirit of 'Seventy-Six*, Vols. 1 & 2. New York: Bobbs Merrill, 1958.

Daniel, Clifton, and John W. Kirshon, eds. *Chronicle of America*. New York: Chronicle Publications, n.d.

Davidson, Marshall. *Life in America*, Vols. 1 & 2. Boston: Houghton Mifflin, 1951.

DePauw, Linda Grant. *Founding Mothers*. Boston: Houghton Mifflin, 1975.

Earle, Alice Morse. *Child Life in Colonial Days*. New York: Macmillan, 1927.

———. *Home Life in Colonial Days*. Reprint, n.d.

Fahey, Frank M., and Marie L. Fahey, eds. *Chapters from the American Experience*, Vol. 1. Englewood Cliffs, N.J.: Prentice-Hall, 1971.

Flexner, James Thomas. *America's Old Masters*. New York: Viking Press, 1939.

Foner, Eric. *Paine and Revolutionary America*. New York: Oxford University Press, 1976.

Gallant, Roy A. *The Peopling of Planet Earth*. New York: Macmillan, 1990.

Griffin, Byckley S., ed. *Offbeat History: A Compendium of Lively Americana*. New York: World, 1967.

Hanaford, Phebe A. *Daughters of America*. Boston: True & Co., 1882. Reprint. *Women of the Century*. Boston: B. B. Russell, n.d.

Handlin, Oscar, and Lilian Handlin. *A Restless People: Americans in Rebellion 1770–1787*. New York: Anchor Books, 1982.

Hart, Albert Bushnell, ed. *American History Told by Contemporaries*, Vol. 2. New York: Macmillan, 1898.

Hughes, Rupert. *George Washington: The Rebel and the Patriot 1762–1777*. New York: William Morrow, 1927.

Ketchum, Richard, ed. *The American Heritage Book of the Revolution*. New York: American Heritage, 1971.

Kinnaird, Clark. *George Washington: The Pictorial Biography*. New York: Hastings House, 1967.

Loeper, John J. *Going to School in 1776*. New York: Atheneum, 1973.

Morgan, Edmund S. *Virginians at Home: Family Life in the Eighteenth Century*. Williamsburg, Va.: Colonial Williamsburg Foundation, 1952.

Morris, Richard B. *Seven Who Shaped Our Destiny*. New York: Harper & Row, 1973.

People's Bicentennial Commission, eds. *Voices of the American Revolution*. New York: Bantam Books, 1975.

"Picturing America 1497–1899." (An Exhibition at the New York Public Library.) *Journal of the American Historical Print Collectors Society*, (13) Autumn 1988: no. 2.

Ressmeyer, Richard H., curator. *Young America*. Sandwich, Mass.: Heritage Plantation, 1985.

Schouler, James. *Americans of 1776: Daily Life during the Revolutionary Period*. Mass.: Corner House Publishers, 1976.

Smith, Carter, ed. *Daily Life; The Arts and Sciences; Governing and Teaching: Three Sourcebooks on Colonial America. American Albums from the Collection of the Library of Congress*. New York: Millbrook Press, n.d.

Smith, Page. *A New Age Begins: A People's History of the American Revolution*, Vols. 1 & 2. New York: Penguin, 1976.

Speare, Elizabeth George. *Life in Colonial America*. New York: Random House, 1963.

Thorp, Willard, Carlos Baker, James K. Folsom, and Merle Curtis, eds. *The American Literary Record*. New York: J. B. Lippincott, 1961.

Wattenberg, Ben, ed. *Statistical History of the United States (Colonial Times to the Present)*. New York: Basic Books, 1976.

Zinn, Howard. *A People's History of the United States*. New York: Harper & Row, 1980.

Picture Credits

Index